Battle of the
Best Friends

★ Also by ★

Debbie Dadey

MERMAID TALES, BOOK 1:
TROUBLE AT TRIDENT ACADEMY

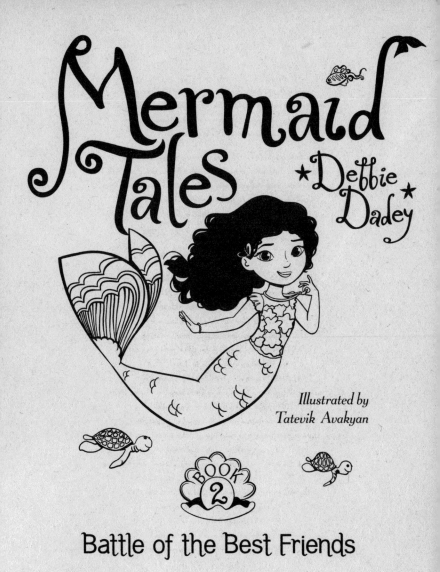

Mermaid Tales

★Debbie Dadey★

Illustrated by
Tatevik Avakyan

BOOK 2

Battle of the Best Friends

ALADDIN
NEW YORK   LONDON   TORONTO   SYDNEY   NEW DELHI

ALADDIN

An imprint of Simon & Schuster Children's Publishing Division

1230 Avenue of the Americas, New York, NY 10020

First Aladdin paperback edition May 2012

Text copyright © 2012 by Debbie Dadey

Illustrations copyright © 2012 by Tatevik Avakyan

All rights reserved, including the right of reproduction
in whole or in part in any form.

ALADDIN is a trademark of Simon & Schuster, Inc.,
and related logo is a registered trademark of Simon & Schuster, Inc.

Also available in an Aladdin hardcover edition.

For information about special discounts for bulk purchases,
please contact Simon & Schuster Special Sales at 1-866-506-1949
or business@simonandschuster.com.

The Simon & Schuster Speakers Bureau can bring authors to your live event.
For more information or to book an event contact
the Simon & Schuster Speakers Bureau at 1-866-248-3049
or visit our website at www.simonspeakers.com.

Designed by Karin Paprocki

The text of this book was set in Belucian Book.

Manufactured in the United States of America 0412 OFF

2 4 6 8 10 9 7 5 3 1

Library of Congress Control Number 2012930531

ISBN 978-1-4424-4979-4 (hc)

ISBN 978-1-4424-2982-6 (pbk)

ISBN 978-1-4424-2983-3 (eBook)

To Nixon Fow,
may you have many adventures
in your third year

* * * *

Acknowledgment

Thanks to my daughter, Becky Dadey,

who brings music to our shell.

Contents

Battle of the Best Friends

1

The News

WHAT IS TAKING SHELLY so long?" Echo asked. She swam back and forth, then peeked around the corner of her shell. If Shelly didn't hurry, they would be late for school.

"Too bad I don't have one of those gadgets humans use to talk to someone who's far away," Echo said.

People fascinated Echo. Ever since Shelly's grandfather had told her about their machines that capture singing, Echo had wanted to see a human. She even wondered what it would be like to *not* have a tail.

She did a huge backward flip and smiled. Having a tail did have *some* advantages. If she kept practicing her flips, she hoped to make the Tail Flippers team at her new school, Trident Academy. Tryouts were this week. Her best friend, Shelly, had already tried out for the Shell Wars sports team at school. Echo did another flip, this time twisting sideways.

"That was great," Shelly said, swimming up beside her.

"There you are!" Echo squealed. "Have you heard the news?"

"Yes!" Shelly shouted. "I can't wait!"

"Me neither," Echo said. "Come on, let's get to school."

The two mergirls splashed past the statues of famous merfolk in MerPark.

"I can't believe Pearl was able to do it," Echo said as they swam quickly along.

Shelly brushed a lock of red hair out of her face. "Pearl?" she asked. "Pearl didn't even try out." Pearl was another mergirl in their third-grade class, who seemed to think she was better than everyone else.

Echo laughed as they reached the

entrance to their school. "You don't have to try out; you just need lots of jewels to pay for them."

"You can *pay* to get on the Shell Wars team?" Shelly asked. "I thought Pearl hated Shell Wars."

Echo stopped and stared at her friend. "*What* are you talking about?"

"I'm talking about Shell Wars. Coach Barnacle announces who made the team today. What are *you* talking about?"

Echo grabbed Shelly's hands and squeezed them tightly. "I'm talking about Pearl's birthday party. She's invited the Rays!"

"You're kidding!" Shelly screamed. There wasn't a merperson alive who hadn't heard of the Rays. They were an amazing boy band and they were very, very cute.

"Didn't you get your invitation?" Echo asked.

Shelly shook her head.

"I bet you'll get it today," Echo told her friend. She smiled as they went into the school, but she was a little worried. Pearl wasn't exactly the nicest mergirl in their class, and she didn't like Shelly very much.

What if Pearl hadn't invited Shelly? What would Echo do?

2

Pearl

I MADE IT!" SHELLY YELLED. SHE AND
Echo had finally gotten to the front
of a long line of merkids outside the
Trident Academy gym. A list had been
posted with the names of this year's Shell
Wars team members.

As soon as Shelly read her name, Rocky

pushed her out of the way. "Move it!" said the merboy, who was in Shelly and Echo's class. "If you made the team, I had to make it too. You stink!"

Echo and Shelly backed away from the list to let the crowd behind them see. Everyone wanted to know who had made their grade's team.

"Congratulations," said Kiki. She was a small, dark-haired mergirl new to Trident City and a new friend of Shelly's.

"You'll be the best Shell Wars player ever," Echo added.

Shelly laughed. "I'd just be happy not getting smacked in the stomach with the shell. But, Kiki, I'm so sorry you didn't make the team."

Kiki shrugged. "It's okay. I've never really played it before, so I knew it was a long shot. I'll join some clubs instead."

"There are some amazing clubs here at Trident Academy," Echo said.

Shelly nodded. "I can't believe our first Shell Wars game is Thursday."

Echo gasped. "That's when the Tail Flippers tryouts are! I wanted to go to your first game."

"I wanted to watch *you* try out," Shelly said. "Maybe I can come during halftime."

"I'll watch," Kiki said, "and cheer for Echo. Next time I'll go to your game, Shelly."

"Thanks," Shelly said. "Echo, I know you'll make the team."

"Right now we'd better get to class," Echo said as the conch shell horn began to sound. All the kids in the hall raced to their classrooms. Echo, Kiki, and Shelly slid into their rock desks just as the final sound blasted. Rocky, who was always late, swam in seconds later.

Pearl was already in class. Echo wanted to ask her about the party. Maybe she hadn't sent out all her invitations yet. Maybe Shelly's got lost in the underwater snail mail. Maybe Pearl didn't know Shelly's address.

Echo was so worried about Shelly and the party, she didn't hear a word anyone said until her teacher, Mrs. Karp, announced, "The report is due on Monday."

Monday? I'll just have to find out later what the assignment is, Echo thought. *I need to speak to Pearl before I do anything!*

Echo finally got the chance to ask Pearl about the party after school at Tail Flippers practice.

"I'll see Shelly later if you want me to give her the invitation," Shelly told Pearl.

"No thanks," Pearl said, gently removing the long strand of pearls she wore around her neck and putting it on a nearby rock. No jewelry was allowed during any after-school sports. "I don't invite icky Shell Wars players to my lovely home."

"But you invited Rocky," Echo said. She had heard Rocky talking about the party in the lunchroom.

Pearl giggled. "I know. He's *so* cute, and we need boys for dancing."

"But Shelly is really nice. You'll find out when you get to know her better," Echo said.

"I know all I want to know," Pearl said with a sniff. "And from now on, if you want to be friends with me, you can't be friends with Shelly."

Awful

I CAN'T BELIEVE PEARL!" SAID SHELLY

the next morning while the girls made their way to school. "Did she really say that?"

Echo nodded sadly. "I told her to take her friendship and feed it to the sea turtles."

Shelly hugged her friend. "Thanks for

sticking up for me," she said. "But I know you've always wanted to see the Rays. You've taught me all of their songs."

Echo laughed. "I bet you sing better than they do." Echo had to admit she was a little bit jealous of Shelly's singing. Every mergirl could sing well, but some had a special gift and sang like sirens of long ago. Shelly had that gift.

"Maybe we should have our own party," Shelly said as the girls swam past MerPark. "We could have a Rays sing-along of our own for everyone who wasn't invited. Kiki told me she didn't get an invitation either."

Echo splashed up and down. "Great idea, Shelly!"

"We *could* do that, but I still think you should go to Pearl's party. I don't have to do everything you do," Shelly said.

"I know," Echo said. "But if I go, it's like I agree with Pearl, and I don't. She shouldn't be so mean."

"But this is the chance of a lifetime," Shelly argued.

Echo shrugged. "Mergirls live very long lives, so I'm sure I'll get another chance to see the Rays."

Shelly didn't say anything. She just nodded.

Zoom! Something rushed past the girls and into Trident Academy.

"What was that?" Echo asked. "It wasn't a shark, was it?" The residents of Trident

City were always on the lookout for sharks. Even though they rarely came into waters this deep, the city had shark patrols that kept constant watch.

"That wasn't a shark," Shelly said. "It was Rocky."

"I can't help it," Echo said with a giggle. "I still think he's awfully cute."

"He's awful, all right," Shelly said, remembering the time he swiped a shrimp she was getting for a project, "but I'm not sure about the cute part."

4

Upside-Down Day

DID YOU WORK ON YOUR famous merperson report?" Shelly asked Echo as they entered the enormous front hallway of Trident Academy. All around them, hundreds of merkids chatted with their friends. A couple of merboys tossed a lemon sponge back and forth until Coach Barnacle told them to stop.

"What report?" Echo said, swimming around a group of giggling tenth-grade mergirls.

"Didn't you hear Mrs. Karp tell us to do a report on a merperson?"

"When did she say that?" Echo asked. She shook her head and ducked when a fourth grader swam over her in a rush to get to class.

Shelly stopped swimming. "Wait a minute," she said. She took a deep breath and faced Echo. "I am working very hard to do my best at Trident. After all, it's a family tradition. My parents and grand-parents all went to school here. It's really,

really important that I do well."

"I know," Echo said. "Don't worry. You'll do great."

Shelly scrunched her nose up. She looked right at Echo and said, "I can't be friends with someone who doesn't even *try* in school."

Echo fell backward in surprise. "What?"

"You heard me," Shelly said. "I thought about it all night, and it's best if we're not friends anymore." And then she swam away.

Echo couldn't believe her ears. *What happened?* How could Shelly treat her this way? They had been best friends for as long as she could remember.

ALL MORNING LONG, SHELLY IGNORED Echo during class. At lunch, Shelly turned her back on Echo and sat at a table for two with Kiki.

"Come sit with us," Pearl said, pulling Echo's pink tail.

Echo sat with Pearl and her friends, but she didn't say a word. Instead, she watched Shelly and Kiki. They looked like they were having a great time without her, talking and laughing. They even walked on their hands in front of Mr. Fangtooth, the cafeteria worker.

"They are trying to make him laugh," Echo said, breaking her silence.

Pearl looked at Mr. Fangtooth. "He's such a grouch. They'll never cheer him up. How ridiculous!"

Echo didn't think it was silly to be nice. In fact, she thought it was the best thing in the world. And more than anything, she wanted to make Mr. Fangtooth laugh with Shelly and Kiki. On the first day

of third grade the mergirls had made crabby-looking Mr. Fangtooth laugh. Even though they had gotten into trouble, they were glad they'd tried to make him happy.

Echo stood up. Shelly looked at her. Immediately Shelly and Kiki rushed back to their table and sat down. Echo couldn't help herself—she quickly swam out of the cafeteria. Then, in the hallway, she cried and cried.

Tryouts

THIS IS SO THRILLING!" PEARL squealed as twenty mergirls lined up for the Tail Flippers tryouts on Thursday. The MerPark stands were full of friends and family who had come to watch the after-school event.

Echo knew she should be excited. After all, she had practiced ever since the first day of school. Her father and mother had taken off work to see her try out. Her older sister, Crystal, even came to watch. Kiki was in the stands supporting her. But all Echo could think about was the way Shelly had treated her. It was the worst time of her life.

Echo was beginning to think that Trident Academy was bad for their friendship. At the beginning of the school year, she and Shelly had an argument about homework. They never used to argue. "I should just go home now," Echo said out loud. "I'm never going to make the team."

Wanda, a mergirl in Echo's class and

Kiki's roommate, frowned. "You'll never make it with that attitude. You have to be confident, Echo."

Echo sighed. She wasn't confident at all. She was way too sad. She missed her friend. But then she heard something that changed everything.

"Good luck, Echo!" someone shouted. Echo looked up in the stands and saw Kiki. And right beside her, *Shelly* held a big seaweed sign that read GO ECHO! in red letters.

Great! Shelly must not be mad anymore, Echo thought, and waved at her friends.

"All right, merladies," announced Coach Barnacle. "Let the tryouts begin."

The Trident Academy Pep Band played

their instruments. Several older mer-students used conch shells to blow tunes while three merboys pounded out a beat on a huge sharkskin drum. Suddenly Coach Barnacle smashed two shells together. "That's our signal," Pearl said.

All twenty mergirls began flipping backward and sideways to the music. The merpeople in the stands clapped along. Echo giggled. It was so much fun. She was doing her best turns and flips. She was happy, but mostly because Shelly was there to support her.

The music stopped and Coach Barnacle chose five girls from the group: Pearl, Echo, and three others Echo didn't know. Echo felt bad for Wanda and the girls who weren't chosen. They had worked just as hard as she had.

"Congratulations! You are the new Tail Flippers team!" Coach said. "We start practice tomorrow after school, so don't be late. See you then."

Echo swam over to her parents and her sister.

"Your flips were fantastic," Crystal said.

"Did you really think so?" Echo asked.

"You'll be a wonderful member of the team," Echo's mother added. "Your father and I have to get back to work, but we'll celebrate at home later."

Echo's family left, and she found Kiki. "Thanks so much for coming," Echo said, hugging her. "Where is Shelly?"

"Who?" Kiki asked.

"I saw Shelly right beside you," Echo said. "I wanted to ask her about her game."

Kiki shrugged. "I heard they won, but I think she's still mad at you."

The smile on Echo's face disappeared. "But she was holding up a good-luck sign. I thought she wasn't angry anymore. Why would she come to cheer me on? Oh, Kiki, how can Shelly and I be friends again?"

Kiki looked down at the sandy ocean floor and twitched her purple tail. "I don't know," she said softly.

All Echo wanted to do was go home and cry. She didn't even care that she had made the Tail Flippers team.

"Bye," Echo said sadly as she floated away from MerPark.

"I'm sorry," Kiki called after her.

I'm sorry too, Echo said to herself. *Why couldn't I have paid attention in class? Then none of this would have happened.*

A soft hand grabbed Echo's arm. "Isn't it totally fabulous?" Pearl asked. "We made the Tail Flippers!"

Echo nodded. "Yeah, it's great."

"You have to come to my house to celebrate," Pearl said. "My mom will make us coconut shakes."

"What's a coconut?" Echo asked.

Pearl laughed. "It's food that humans eat. It looks like a big, round ball and grows on this thing called a tree on land.

Sometimes the coconuts fall into the ocean. They are very rare and quite delicious."

Echo shook her head. "Thanks, but . . ."

Pearl wouldn't take no for an answer. "You have to come. We can celebrate and work on our famous merperson assignment for Monday. We have a whole merlibrary filled with lots of stories. And I'll tell you all about my party!"

Echo was so upset about losing Shelly as a friend that she decided to go with Pearl. "All right," Echo said halfheartedly. After all, she did need to do her report.

PEARL LIVED IN THE BIGGEST HOME IN Shell Estates. It was almost as big as Trident Academy. Her shell's ceiling was

lined with hundreds of different-colored jellyfish lamps. A spectacular seaweed curtain hung beside a curving marble staircase. The curtain and staircase were encrusted with thousands of gleaming jewels.

"Your home is beautiful," Echo said.

"I know," Pearl said. "We might get a bigger one next year."

As the mergirls swam into a massive rock library, Echo couldn't imagine anyone needing a bigger shell. Pearl's home *was* nice, but the only place Echo wanted to be was with Shelly at the apartment she shared with her grandfather above the People Museum.

Echo wondered if she'd ever get the chance to be there again.

Kiki's Secret

EVERYONE'S TAILS ARE GLEAMING," Pearl said to Echo the next day at lunch. "I told them they had to polish themselves if they wanted to come to my party tonight."

Echo glanced at her own tail. It was looking a bit dull. "I'll shine mine later."

Pearl looked down her pointy nose at Echo. "Well, I should hope so. It's too bad we have Tail Flippers practice after school. I wonder if Coach Barnacle would excuse me since it's my birthday."

Echo shrugged. "It is our first official practice."

Pearl rolled her eyes. "I know. We can't miss it or we'll get kicked off the team. Maybe I shouldn't have even tried out! What's more important than my birthday?" She swam away to buy her lunch. She had told Echo she always chose the black-lip oyster and sablefish stew because it was the most expensive item on the menu.

Echo sighed and looked down at her hagfish jelly sandwich. She wasn't hungry, but merpeople never wasted food. It was too precious. So she slowly chewed every last bite. She was surprised that Pearl hadn't come back to their table yet. When Echo looked around, she saw Pearl sticking her tongue out at Mr. Fangtooth. But she wasn't doing it to make him laugh, she was doing it to be cruel.

Echo jumped up from the table. She had to stop Pearl from being so mean! She started to rush over to Mr. Fangtooth when—*slam!*—she collided with Kiki, right in the middle of the lunchroom. Everyone stopped eating and stared at them. Rocky and a few other boys laughed.

"Mergirl sea wreck," Rocky joked.

Echo's cheeks turned red.

"I'm sorry," Kiki told Echo.

"Me too," Echo said. "I didn't see you coming."

"I need to tell you something now, while Shelly is in the art room," Kiki said softly. "She's working on a special project, and I have to go help her. I should have told you this yesterday, but Shelly doesn't want you to know."

Echo put her right hand on her hip. "I already know what you're going to say: Shelly is *still* mad at me."

Kiki shook her head. "No, Echo. Shelly isn't mad at all."

"Yes, she is. She's been mean to me all week. She hasn't spoken to me once," Echo said.

"Shelly is only *pretending* to be angry," Kiki said. "She knows you want to see the Rays at Pearl's party. But you're such a good friend, you won't go unless she's invited too. Don't tell her I told you! After today—when the party is over—she'll try to be friends again. I hope you'll let her."

Kiki swam away and Echo was left with her mouth open in surprise. Was Kiki telling the truth?

Non-Rays Party

ECHO WAS DYING TO TALK TO Shelly during class, but Mrs. Karp kept them too busy all afternoon. After school Shelly was nowhere to be found, and Echo had Tail Flippers practice.

"Oh my Neptune!" Pearl said at MerPark. "Just think, in a few short hours we are actually going to see the Rays—all because of me!"

The other girls on the team squealed in delight, but Echo just smiled. She had to admit, it was pretty amazing that such a famous group would be in Trident City.

It was hard for the team to concentrate on practice. Pearl forgot to take off her necklace and got her tail tangled up. It took the first half of practice just to unsnarl her. Then Pearl's and Echo's tails collided and they both crashed to the ocean floor.

Finally Coach Barnacle gave up, threw his hands in the air, and said, "Girls, go

home. Hopefully we'll have better luck at the next practice."

"Yes!" shouted Pearl. "I'm going home to put on my new outfit."

"Bye!" Echo said, zooming off as fast as she could. She didn't head home to polish the scales on her tail. She didn't head home to change into party clothes. She swam right past her shell to Shelly's apartment at the People Museum.

"Watch it!" snapped an old merwoman, who was moving slowly toward Manta Ray Station.

"Sorry," Echo called, zipping around the merlady and her wolffish.

"Merkids think they own the entire ocean," the merwoman muttered. The startled wolffish hid behind a rock until the old merwoman coaxed it out.

Echo found Shelly in her room, resting on a bath sponge. "Congratulations on winning your first Shell Wars game," Echo said. "I'm sorry I didn't get to see it, but I did make the Tail Flippers team. I saw you cheering for me in the stands."

"Echo!" Shelly screamed. "What are you doing here? Why aren't you at Pearl's shell?"

"Because I want to be with a *real* friend," Echo said.

"But . . . I'm not your friend. Not any-more," Shelly said slowly.

Echo laughed. "I know better. You were only pretending to be mad so I would go to the party."

Shelly's face turned red. "How did you find out? Did Kiki tell you?"

"Don't blame Kiki," Echo said. "You are more important to me than any silly band."

"But I know you wanted to see the Rays. That's why I made up the story about you not trying hard enough in class," Shelly said.

"But I'd rather be your friend than see any boy band," Echo said.

Shelly hugged Echo. "Are you sure?"

"I'm sure." Echo knew she was doing the right thing. "Let's go to the Big Rock Café for a colossal kelp drink," Echo said. "We can celebrate your Shell Wars victory and my making the Tail Flippers."

"The two of us can celebrate another

day. Right now it's time for the party at the Big Rock Café."

"You decided to have the sing-along anyway?" Echo asked.

"Yes," Shelly explained. "Kiki and I made signs to let everyone who wasn't invited to Pearl's party know about our celebration at the Big Rock."

"So that's what you were doing in the art room when I was talking to Kiki. What a good idea," Echo said.

"Let's go!" Shelly said. The two girls sped off to the café. When they swam in the doorway, they couldn't believe their eyes!

8

Great Wasp Tragedy

SITTING AT THE ROCK COUNTER were the Rays. All four of them! Hanging above them was a sign that said WHO NEEDS THE RAYS? LET'S MAKE OUR OWN MUSIC! Everyone in the Big Rock Café stared at the boy band, even the merwaitresses and mercooks.

Kiki rushed over to Shelly and Echo. "I thought this was a party *without* the Rays. How did you get the most famous band in the ocean to come here?"

Echo held up her palms in surprise. Shelly shrugged and said, "We didn't do anything, but there's one way to find out."

"You're going to talk to them?" Kiki asked, barely whispering.

"Of course. They're only merpeople," Shelly said.

"But they're stars," Echo whimpered. "They probably don't even *speak* to ordinary mergirls like us."

"Well, if they don't, it will be a short

conversation," Shelly said, pulling Echo toward the Rays. Kiki swam along, hiding behind Echo.

"Excuse me," Shelly said. "I'm Shelly. These are my friends Echo and Kiki. It's cool you're here, but aren't you supposed to be at Pearl's party?"

A handsome merboy not much older than Shelly leaped off his rock stool. "Greetings, merladies. Lovely to meet you. I'm Alden, and this is Harmon," he said in a strange accent. "You're right. We are supposed to be at a party, but there's a problem."

Harmon, an even cuter merboy, put a hand on Alden's shoulder. "Our backup singer was stung by a sea wasp today. It was horrible."

"Oh no!" Kiki said, sticking her head

out from behind Echo. "Sea wasps are so

poisonous. Is your singer okay?"

Alden shook his head. "Doc Weedly says Gwen will be better in a week. But she can't sing a bubble until she gets well." Alden pointed to two other band members. "Teddy and Ellis sing, but we still need a mergirl's voice."

"I'm so sorry about your singer," Echo said to the band. She couldn't believe she was having a conversation with Alden of the Rays!

"We'd like to honor our commitment to Pearl, but we can't go on without Gwen, even though she wants us to," Alden told them.

Shelly nodded. "It's too bad. Pearl is going to be terribly disappointed. You're all she's been talking about this week."

Echo couldn't believe her ears. After all, Pearl hadn't even invited Shelly to the party. But then Echo had an idea. It was a totally fabulous, crazy idea.

"You know," Echo said, "I know someone who is a super singer. And she knows every word to every one of your songs."

"Really? Who is it? Where is she?" the Rays said together.

Echo put her arm around Shelly's shoulders and said, "She's right here. It's Shelly!"

Shelly jerked away from Echo. "Are you shell-shocked? I can't do that!"

Alden grabbed Shelly's hand and said, "Why not? Let's do it. It will be a blast!"

Shelly backed away. "No way! I can't go to Pearl's party. I wasn't invited."

Teddy piped up, "You're invited now. You're part of the band."

"But I'm having a sing-along here for my friends," Shelly explained,

NON-RAYS PARTY

pointing to the sign above their heads. "I can't leave them behind." The Rays looked around the Big Rock Café. Kiki and then other kids waved shyly at the band.

"Sorry about the sign. We really do like you," Kiki explained.

The Rays looked above them and grinned at the words WHO NEEDS THE RAYS?

"Guess what?" Alden said to the kids in the café. "You're all coming to Pearl's party as our guests. We'll rock together. Are you with us?"

9

Pearl's Party Crashers

I CAN'T BELIEVE IT! YOU'RE REALLY here!" Pearl shrieked when she saw the Rays. "Please come in," she said, pointing the way inside her grand shell.

"Great," Alden said. "We hope you don't mind that we brought a few friends of ours too."

Pearl giggled. "Any friends of yours are welcome."

"Totally cool. Come on, guys." The four Rays stood by as Shelly, Kiki, Echo, and all the kids from the Big Rock Café floated toward Pearl's home. Pearl's mouth dropped open when she saw who was with the band.

"You aren't invited to this party," Pearl snapped at Shelly, and blocked the entrance to her home.

"She's part of the band," Alden explained, swimming up beside Shelly. "Our backup singer was stung by a sea wasp, and Shelly is helping us out."

Harmon piped up, "Of course, we'd understand if you'd rather we cancel. We have had a very hard day."

"Oh no, you can't cancel," Pearl said quickly. Pearl frowned at Shelly, but moved out of the way. "Everyone can come on in."

In a few short minutes the Rays had set up their instruments on the huge marble staircase in Pearl's entryway.

"Are you sure I can do this?" Shelly asked Echo.

Echo hugged her friend. "I know you can."

Shelly took a deep breath and swam between Alden, Harmon, Teddy, and Ellis.

"Shark, the sharpnose sevengill, lived near to me. We swam together every day and became

the best of friends," Teddy sang, and all the girls in the audience screamed, even Kiki and Echo.

"*Best of friends,*" sang Shelly.

"Go, Shelly!" yelled Echo.

"*Then someone told Shark he should eat me. And now I miss him terribly,*" sang Teddy. "*But our friendship had to end.*"

"*Had to end,*" sang Shelly.

"*Shark, the sharpnose sevengill, lived near to me,*" sang Ellis. "*I'll always treasure our friendship. And hope someday he'll see . . .*"

Then Teddy and Ellis leaned together and motioned for Shelly to join them. "*That sharks and merfolks can be friends. One day it will be.*"

Shelly repeated, "*One day it will be.*"

Then the Rays and Shelly finished the song. *"But until that day I guess I'll say, 'Shark, I miss you still.'"*

"I miss you still!" Shelly sang in the most amazing high voice.

Kiki grinned as everyone cheered. "Shelly is really good."

Echo nodded. She knew Shelly would be.

When the song ended, all the merkids clapped wildly. Then Alden pointed to Pearl.

"Happy birthday to Pearl. We want to thank you for inviting us."

"Thank Shelly!" Kiki yelled. "Without her, there'd be no show."

Alden laughed. "That's right. Let's hear it for Shelly." Everyone cheered as Shelly waved and the Rays started a new song.

"Do you think Pearl will be mad you said that?" Echo asked Kiki.

Kiki shook her head. "Any other mergirl would thank Shelly for helping. Without her, the party would have been canceled."

"Pearl's not like anyone else. That's for sure," Echo whispered to Kiki. "Look."

Echo pointed to Pearl. Pearl wasn't cheering. And she wasn't singing along to the music. She was glaring right at Shelly.

Star

SHELLY, YOU'RE A STAR!" WANDA told Shelly at school on Monday.

Shelly's face turned bright red. "It was a lot of fun, but I was so afraid I'd mess up."

"It was the most amazing party ever," Kiki added. "I didn't want the Rays to leave."

Shelly nodded. "They were so nice."

"You mean you actually got to talk to them?" another mergirl asked. Almost every merkid in class gathered around Shelly.

Shelly nodded. "Echo, Kiki, and I all did."

Pearl sniffed. "I talked to them too," she said.

"Alden is *sooooo* cute," a girl named Morgan whispered.

Echo giggled. "He even held Shelly's hand." Several girls almost fainted, so it was a good thing Mrs. Karp swooped into the room. "Class, please turn in your merperson assignments."

Everyone except for Rocky passed in his or her report.

"Rocky, where is yours?" asked Mrs. Karp.

Rocky shrugged. "A killer whale stole it from me on the way to school."

Mrs. Karp nodded and said, "Tomorrow you may turn in your merperson report as well as one on killer whales."

Rocky slouched down in his chair while Mrs. Karp glanced over the seaweed pages. "Hmm, this is strange. Pearl's and Echo's stories begin the exact same way."

Echo gasped and looked at Pearl. Did Pearl copy her report when they'd worked at her house? Pearl turned red and looked down at her desk. She played with her long necklace and wouldn't look at Echo. Thankfully, Mrs. Karp didn't say anything else about the stories and pointed to a big chart on the wall showing different kinds of whales.

Later at lunch, Pearl swam over to Shelly and said, "You're a star all because of me and my party! Why don't you sit at *my* table today?"

Echo couldn't believe Pearl! She was so angry with her. Pearl not only copied her story, now she was trying to take away Echo's friend. Would Shelly go with Pearl?

"Thanks," Shelly said, "but Kiki and Echo liked me even when I didn't sing with the Rays, so I'll sit with them."

"Suit yourself," Pearl snapped. "Sit with those bottom-feeders."

"They aren't bottom-feeders," Shelly

said. "Kiki and Echo are amazing mergirls, and if it wasn't for them, the Rays wouldn't have been at your party. Echo's idea saved the day."

Pearl stuck her nose up in the air. "Humph," she said, before rushing off to her table.

"She makes me mad enough to scream," Shelly said.

"Don't scream, Shelly." Echo giggled. "You'll ruin your voice!"

Echo pulled Shelly toward another table. "And don't worry about Pearl," Echo said. "The three of us are best friends, and that makes us winners."

Kiki nodded. "Winners every time."

Class Reports

**THE STORY OF
MARIS**

By Shelly Siren

Maris ruled the
sea many years ago, when Trident City
was first built. She rode a killer whale and
traveled freely among the many merpeople
and ocean animals. Not only was she
kind and fair, but she made peace with the

sharks by offering them their own hunting grounds. Once she was challenged by an evil merman who lunged at her with a sharp whalebone. She called out to all her animal friends for help. In a flash, the evil merman was eaten by a shark. Maris recovered and ruled for many more years.

THE STORY OF ALANNA

By Echo Reef

Alanna lived in ancient times, before Trident City was even built. She had a beautiful voice and often tricked human sailors into following her. One sailor happened to see her when his ship sank. He fell in love with her. Alanna saved him, but after that she never teased sailors again. It is believed she fell in love with the sailor, and that is what made her seek to pass the merfolk law to never taunt human sailors.

THE STORY OF MERLIN

By Rocky Ridge

Merlin may or may not have been a merperson. He lived with the merfolk for many years and showed them much magic. He may have used his magic to become a merman. Magic means making something extraordinary happen. Merlin could wave a wand when he was hungry and make a school of fish appear. He could talk with sharks and is believed to be the only merman to ever ride a great white.

MY REPORT ON KILLER WHALES

By Rocky Ridge

Killer whales do not normally eat seaweed school reports, but it is possible. Usually they eat fish, squid, birds, seals, and even other whales. They are big and black and white.

THE STORY OF ALANNA

By Pearl Swamp

I HAD TO DO IT OVER!

Many years ago, before Trident City was even built, there was a beautiful mermaid named Alanna. Everything about her was beautiful, even her voice, and she liked to tease human sailors into following her. One sailor happened to see her when he fell out of his ship. He loved her. Alanna saved him, but after that she never teased sailors again. She fell in love with the sailor and that is what made her pass a law to never taunt human sailors, which, if you ask me, is a stupid law. And why would any mermaid fall in love with a human? I mean, humans don't even have tails! EWWW!

THE STORY OF MAPELLA

By Kiki Coral

Thousands of years ago near the South China Sea, a young mermaid named Mapella was born. Mapella traveled more than any merperson before her had ever dared. She loved seeing new places, but she also carved maps of everywhere she went. In the ancient mercity of Dao-Ming, visitors can still see the reliefs Mapella made. She was the first mapmaker, or cartographer, of the merpeople. She gave her name to the maps we still use today. Her traveling stopped when she was eaten by a tiger shark.

The Mermaid Song

REFRAIN:

Let the water roar

Deep down we're swimming along

Twirling, swirling, singing the mermaid song.

VERSE 1:

Shelly flips her tail

Racing, diving, chasing a whale

Twirling, swirling, singing the mermaid song.

VERSE 2:

Pearl likes to shine

Oh my Neptune, she looks so fine

Twirling, swirling, singing the mermaid song.

VERSE 3:

Shining Echo flips her tail

Backward and forward without fail

Twirling, swirling, singing the mermaid song.

VERSE 4:

Amazing Kiki

Far from home and floating so free

Twirling, swirling, singing the mermaid song.

Shark, the Sharpnose Sevengill

Shark, the sharpnose sevengill,

lived near to me

We swam together every day

and became the best of friends

Then someone told Shark

he should eat me

And now I miss him terribly

But our friendship had to end

Shark, the sharpnose sevengill,

lived near to me

I'll always treasure our friendship

And hope someday he'll see

That sharks and merfolks can be friends

One day it will be

But until that day I guess I'll say,

"Shark, I miss you still."

Author's Note

THE OCEAN IS AN AMAZING place full of secrets. There are many places underwater that have yet to be investigated by humans. Maybe one day, explorers will find a mermaid band deep on the ocean floor. Read the next pages to find out about some other amazing ocean life. I hope you'll let me know your favorite creature. You can write to me on Kids Talk at www.debbiedadey.com.

Swim free,

Debbie Dadey

Glossary

BARNACLE: A barnacle is a crustacean that sticks itself to boats or other creatures, like whales.

BATH SPONGE: The Mediterranean bath sponge is not common today because in the past, huge numbers were caught by humans and used for cleaning and bathing.

BLACK-LIP OYSTER: The black-lip pearl oyster begins life as a male and changes into a female! It sometimes produces black pearls.

COCONUT: The coconut grows on palm trees in warm climates on land. The coconut, shaped like a big brown soccer ball, has been known to get caught in ocean currents and travel great distances. It will float and it is waterproof. The inside of a coconut contains sweet liquid.

CORAL: Coral polyps are small, soft-bodied creatures that are related to jellyfish. Coral makes reefs by attaching itself to rocks and dividing. Some of the coral reefs on earth began growing fifty million years ago.

CONCH SHELL: Conch are a kind of marine mollusk that have a heavy spiral shell. In the past, jewelry makers used the shells to carve cameos.

GREAT WHITE SHARK: The great white shark is very smart and can grow up to twenty-four feet, as long as a telephone pole is tall.

HAGFISH: This long, eel-like fish can actually tie itself into knots. It does so quite often, in fact, to help it get rid of the slime that comes out of its pores.

KILLER WHALES: Killer whales (or orcas) are not whales at all, but dolphins. They live together in pods of about twenty for their entire life.

LEMON SEA SPONGE: This bright yellow sponge grows in shallow waters of the Pacific Ocean.

MANTA RAY: They are the largest rays in the ocean, and they are related to sharks. But they are not dangerous—they don't have a stinging spine.

SABLEFISH: Adult sablefish are found in deep waters and sometimes live to be ninety years old!

SEA TURTLES: Sea turtles have been on the earth for 120 million years! Leatherback sea turtles can weigh more than two thousand pounds.

SEA WASP: The sea wasp is another name for the box jellyfish, which is the world's most venomous marine animal. It lives near Australia.

SHARPNOSE SEVENGILL SHARK: This shark is on the endangered species list and lives in deep water. It usually eats squid, crustaceans, and fish near seabeds.

TIGER SHARK: The tiger shark is the second most dangerous shark to humans, after the great white. Tiger sharks will eat almost anything, even garbage. They like coastal waters.

WOLFFISH: This creepy-looking fish is usually found near rocky reefs in deep water. It grows new teeth every year.

FIND OUT WHAT HAPPENS IN THE NEXT . . .

Mermaid Tales

★ Debbie Dadey ★

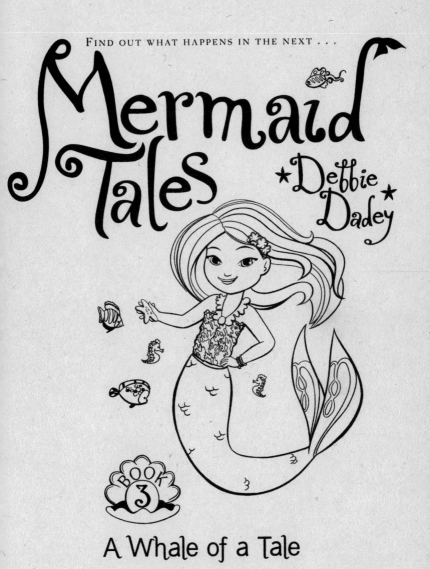

BOOK 3

A Whale of a Tale

Ocean Trip

ROCKY RIDGE WASN'T HAPPY. "Do we have to do another project?" he whined to his teacher. "Mrs. Karp, that's not fair!"

In the first few weeks of the new school year at Trident Academy, Mrs. Karp's third-grade class had already completed reports on famous merpeople and a project where they'd collected krill and shrimp. Every one of the twenty students hoped they wouldn't have to do another big assignment.

Mrs. Karp smiled. "This assignment is different. We're going on an ocean trip."

Rocky and the rest of the class cheered. "Yes! Ocean trip!"

Kiki Coral gasped. But her mer-girl friends Echo Reef and Shelly Siren clapped their hands and swished their tails. For many in the class, this would be their first ocean trip. They would leave classwork behind to learn in the deep-sea environment. "It's about time we did something fun," a mergirl named Pearl Swamp snapped.

"Where are we going, Mrs. Karp?" Kiki asked.

"An article in the *Trident City Tide* reported that a pod of whales is expected to be directly above Trident City tomorrow morning," Mrs. Karp said. "We will visit them. In fact, Dr. Evan Mousteau will join us in a few minutes to tell us about whales and even teach us a bit of whale language."

Mrs. Karp continued, "I expect you to be courteous to Dr. Mousteau. After he leaves, we'll go over surface safety rules. Your parents can feel secure that the

Shark Patrol will be on the alert all morning, not only for sharks, but also for any sign of humans."

Echo could barely speak. "Humans!" she whispered to Shelly and Kiki. "I've always wanted to see a real, live human. Maybe tomorrow will be my chance!" Everything about humans fascinated Echo.

"My parents have never let me go above water. Are you sure it's safe?" Echo asked Mrs. Karp.

Mrs. Karp patted Echo on the shoulder. "Don't worry, we will not go if it's not safe."

Then Kiki shyly asked, "Which whale dialect will we be learning?"

Mrs. Karp raised her green eyebrows. "Excellent question. I wonder how many of you even know that whales talk to one another?"

No one raised their hand except Shelly. Kiki smiled at her.

"Since the visiting pod is made up of humpbacks, we will focus on the humpback whale dialect," Mrs. Karp told the class.

Kiki nodded, still smiling, but in truth she was worried. Really worried.

Dr. Mousteau

DR. MOUSTEAU REMINDED Kiki of the bottlenose dolphins that lived near her home in the far-off waters near Asia. He had the same shiny bald head and long pointed noise. Even his eyes were round and black. Kiki wondered if Dr. Mousteau had twenty-five pairs of teeth in each jaw. When he opened his mouth, she got her answer: He had one big tooth in the center of his top gum. That was it.

"The humpback whale is a wondrous creature," Dr. Mousteau told the third graders. "The pattern of white markings on the flukes and flippers is different on each and every whale. So no two whales are alike."

Dr. Mousteau continued, "Adult humpbacks are quite large and weigh ten times more than a great white shark."

"Those whales need to go on a diet," Rocky blurted out.

Mrs. Karp frowned, but Dr. Mousteau didn't seem to mind Rocky's interruption.

He went on, "As you might know, man is the only predator of whales. Thankfully, humans' captures of whales in recent years have decreased. Still, the humpback population is about one-fifth of what it was hundreds of years ago."

Dr. Mousteau reached into a bag and took out a thick piece of skin. "I'd like each of you to touch the specimen I'm passing around. This was taken from a whale that died naturally. I brought it for you to study."

Dr. Mousteau gave the skin to Rocky, who touched and even sniffed it. Rocky tried to give it to Pearl, but she shook her head. "I don't want to touch any disgusting dead whale. It has awful bumps and nasty barnacles on it."

"That's quite normal," Dr. Mousteau said, taking the specimen and handing it to Shelly. "Every humpback has a long head with knobs such as these. If you didn't clean yourselves thoroughly, you'd have barnacles too."

"I had a barnacle one time," Rocky said, "but my dad made me wash it off."

Shelly felt the whale skin and tried to give it to Kiki, but Kiki's eyes were glued to Dr. Mousteau. "Here, Kiki," Shelly said, but Kiki wouldn't look.

Debbie Dadey

is the author and coauthor of one hundred and fifty children's books, including the series The Adventures of the Bailey School Kids. A former teacher and librarian, Debbie now lives in Bucks County, Pennsylvania, with her wonderful husband and children. They live about two hours from the ocean and love to go there to look for mermaids. If you see any, let her know at www.debbiedadey.com.